SHELKA
THE MIGHTY FORTRESS

With special thanks to Janet Bingham

For Becky

ORCHARD BOOKS

First published in Great Britain in 2016 by The Watts Publishing Group

3 5 7 9 10 8 6 4 2

Text © 2016 Beast Quest Limited.
Cover and inside illustrations by Artful Doodlers with special thanks to Bob and Justin
© Orchard Books 2016

Series created by Beast Quest Limited, London

A CIP catalogue record for this book is available from the British Library.

ISBN 978 1 40834 093 6

Printed and bound by CPI Group (UK) Ltd, Croydon, CR0 4YY

MIX
Paper from
responsible sources
FSC® C104740
www.fsc.org

The paper and board used in this book are made from wood from responsible sources

Orchard Books
An imprint of Hachette Children's Group
Part of The Watts Publishing Group Limited
Carmelite House, 50 Victoria Embankment, London EC4Y 0DZ

An Hachette UK Company
www.hachette.co.uk
www.hachettechildrens.co.uk

SHELKA
THE MIGHTY FORTRESS

BY ADAM BLADE

ORCHARD

WAR IS COMING TO THE DELTA QUADRANT!

For too long I have hidden in exile, watching as Gustados, the greatest of all civilisations, becomes weak.

I have swum amongst the Merryn of Sumara in disguise as one of them, and stolen their secrets. I have walked into Aquora, Arctiria, Verdula and Gustados, invisible to any around me. Now I know how to destroy them.

Deception is the greatest weapon. With it I will make the so-called Delta Quadrant Alliance tear itself apart! And in its place, the Empire of Gustados will rise, with me as its leader – Kade, the Lord of Illusion!

CHAPTER ONE

DOUBTS AND DISTRUST

Sweat ran into Max's eyes as he walked over the scorching sand, heading for the Verdulan coastline. His metal dogbot, Rivet, was trying to escape the sun by padding in Max's shadow. Next to him, Lia was breathing hard, clearly keen to get back to the water. The Merryn princess wasn't used to being on land in such heat.

Max blinked away the moisture and gave one last look back to the group of Verdulans watching them from a distance, with the six Gustadians they'd managed to capture. The Verdulan chief, Naybor, gave a final wave to Max and Lia.

He's the only Verdulan who doesn't want us off their island, thought Max. *Or safely locked up in one of their dungeons.*

"I can't believe they still think we're enemies," said Lia. "Even after we defeated Fangor."

Max frowned. "After Kade's trickery, they don't trust anyone." Since the villainous Gustadian criminal and weapons scientist had set off a bomb at the Alliance's peace conference, all the races of the Delta Quadrant were deeply suspicious of each other. Max felt a shiver pass down his spine as he thought of Kade still on the loose, in command of two more Robobeasts. Kade had awoken the ancient sea creatures from the Merryn temple at Deepholm, using a ring he stole from Sumara that had belonged to Lia's mother. And Kade had added robotics to make the creatures incredibly deadly.

We need to track him down, thought Max. The problem was, they had no idea where he was planning to strike next.

Unless…

His eyes fell on the Gustadian captives, trussed to poles.

"I need to question Kade's minions," he said to Lia. "They might have information."

Lia raised her eyebrows. "I don't know," she said, glancing at the Verdulans. "Naybor's people won't like it."

Max gritted his teeth. "If we don't find Kade, it won't matter who the Verdulans trust, because he'll have taken over the whole Quadrant."

"Okay," said Lia, "but let's be careful."

They walked back up the beach together
and the Verdulans began jabbering in
their strange tongue. Disguised with his
holographic suit, Kade had convinced the
people of Verdula that he was their shaman.
They probably felt a bit humiliated now.
A few poked the air with their spears and
glowered, but Naybor held out a hand and
let Max and Lia approach with Rivet.

Max pointed at the nearest bound Gustadian. "Tell me where Kade has gone," he commanded.

The prisoner laughed. "You are powerless!" he replied. "There's nothing you can do to stop Kade conquering the Quadrant. Why should we help you?"

"Well," said Max. "Here's one good reason: the only thing stopping the Verdulan people from roasting you all alive and eating you for breakfast is our friend Naybor here." The Gustadian shuddered, and Max smiled. "If you help me, I'll put in a good word for you..."

"And why should we trust you?"

Max shrugged. "Fine. Don't." He nodded at Naybor. *"Bon appetit."*

"He's heading for the city of ice!" spat another prisoner.

"You fool!" said the first captive. "Kade will kill us!"

Max grinned. That could only mean Arctiria, the island city built out of a giant iceberg. Max and Lia had fought Nephro the Ice Lobster on its icy towers, while the fussy Arctirians did nothing but complain about the battle-damage to their beautiful city.

"What plan does Kade have for the Actirian people?" Max asked.

The Gustadian who'd spilled the beans just shrugged. "Our master is a genius. We do not need to know his exact plans. Kade asks only that we follow him unquestioningly."

Max tried to read the Gustadian's pale, taught features. *I think he's telling the truth.*

Suddenly, the Gustadian seemed to flicker. For the blink of an eye he looked like a Verdulan. One of the real Verdulans hit him with his spear, and the Gustadian grunted, his shape solidifying again.

They're still wearing their shape-shifter suits, thought Max. Grudgingly, he marvelled at Kade's technological genius. At first glance the suits looked like normal black overalls, but they were ridged with wiring and dotted with tiny nodules. The nodules projected a holographic image around the wearer. "Take off your stealth suits," Max ordered the prisoners. "Don't try anything silly – not if you want Naybor to spare your lives."

Sullenly, with help from the Verdulans, the bound Gustadians wriggled out of the holographic shape-shifter suits. They were wearing armoured deepsuits underneath.

Max turned to Naybor. "You won't kill them, will you?"

Naybor let out a series of jabbering calls and Lia translated. "They will be spared. Naybor is going to lock them up in the dungeon at the centre of one of their pyramids."

Max nodded. "Wait for us on Spike," he said to Lia. "I'll check over the aquasphere with Rivet, then come and meet you. We're heading north."

Lia ran down the beach, calling to Spike. Immediately, the swordfish's dorsal fin broke the surface of the water. Lia dived in and swam out towards him.

Max shook the sand out of the six stealth

suits and bundled them under one arm.
"Let's go, Riv!"

"Yes, Max." Rivet trotted over the beach,
and Max followed him to the shallows where
the aquasphere lay in a tangle of seaweed. He
rolled the transparent plexiglass globe over

in the warm tropical water. Carefully, he inspected the surface, rubbing his sleeve over the grubbiest parts. It looked pretty battered from its mad rush through the jungle, but there were no cracks in the plexiglass. One pair of guns was damaged, half-eaten away by the acid from Kade's mine-fish.

But there's still a set of blasters on the other side. And the hull's watertight.

Max threw the stealth suits inside then jumped into the padded cockpit, followed by Rivet. He tested the controls and checked the holoscreens before coasting out over the surface of the water. *Thrusters working. Engines good.*

"Let's go!" said Max. He revved the engine, zooming away into deeper water with Lia and Spike in their wake. He flicked the switch on the craft's comms device, to call his father. Callum North was the Chief

Defence Engineer of Aquora, and Max hoped he would have some good news about the Delta Quadrant Alliance.

Maybe Dad's helped everyone see sense. Once they know that Kade's the real enemy, they'll stop blaming each other!

"Dad," he said over the intercom. "Are you there? Come in..." But Max heard only static and a sudden loud, high-pitched whine. He flinched away from the speaker. *What's going on?*

A voice echoed through the aquasphere. "Hello, Max."

The hair lifted on the back of Max's neck as he recognised the mocking tone. "Kade!"

"Indeed. I'm using my special radio beacon to block all communications within the Delta Quadrant. I'm in control of the airwaves now." He chuckled. "Of course, that means everyone will be even more suspicious of each other."

"You won't get away with this!" Max said,
through clenched teeth.

Kade laughed. "No? Oh, I know you're
the boy hero of Aquora, Max. I know you
defeated the Professor and his wretched son,
Siborg. But don't fool yourself that you can
beat me! Your old enemies had impressive
weapons, but I am both a tech genius and

the Lord of Illusion. You stand no chance!"

"I wouldn't be too sure," replied Max. "I'll find you..."

"Perhaps you will, Max, but no matter. More and more Gustadians see me as their rightful leader. When the Delta Quadrant erupts into all-out war, I will lead Gustados to victory. The new Empire of Gustados will rule the Delta Quadrant, and I will be its emperor!" With one final mad laugh, Kade's voice vanished.

ICEBERG HIDEAWAY

Max felt frustration bubble up inside him, and he thumped a fist against the console.

"Kade's blocked all Quadrant-wide comms, Lia," he said through his headset.

Lia's eyes widened, then her brow furrowed in worry. "It's one more step in his plan to cause enough chaos to start a war!"

Max nodded. "We need to find him and make him confess to setting off the bomb.

Once we prove that he's the one behind all the trouble, everyone will stop blaming each other."

"No time to lose, then," said Lia.

Max nodded. He gunned the aquasphere's thrusters and powered northwards. "Full speed ahead. Next stop, Arctiria!"

They soon left the waters of Verdula behind them. Max watched as the seascape changed under the clear bottom of the sub, the tropical plants, coral and colourful fish disappearing. Rivet went into rest mode, quiet except for a little dogbot dream-yap every now and then. Every hour that went past, Max knew that the Delta Quadrant came closer to war.

After a while Max noticed Lia rubbing her arms. "What's wrong?" he asked.

"The sea is getting cold," replied Lia. "Very cold, very quickly."

Max tapped the dials on the console.

"That's odd. The instruments say we're still a long way from Arctiria. We haven't even passed Gustados yet. The sea here should still be pretty warm."

Lia shrugged. "Perhaps your Breather tech has made a mistake."

Lia didn't trust technology, but Max did. *If the sea feels cold this far south, then something weird is happening!*

Max spotted something looming in the distance. It looked like a colossal, upside-down mountain, reaching up above the sea's surface. "And there's another thing that doesn't belong here!"

Lia followed his gaze. "An iceberg! And look, there's another, off to the left."

Max shook his head. "It's like the climate's going wrong. And I bet Kade has something to do with it!"

Soon a darker, craggier shape loomed up

ahead. Max recognised the black bedrock. "Gustados," he said to Lia. "We don't have time to stop here." He skirted the aquasphere around the island. Suddenly, the console instruments flashed a warning, and Rivet stirred.

"Sub ahead, Max," he barked.

"I see it, Riv." A large submarine, painted in a riot of rainbow colours, appeared from behind a rocky outcrop. It looked as pretty as a child's toy, but Max knew it was a Gustadian battle sub.

He slowed the aquasphere and tried to hail the submarine with his radio communicator, but there was only static.

Kade's still blocking the comms. I must get through to them before they attack us.

Max edged the aquasphere closer, trying to get within range to use his headset. He held up one hand, palm open, waving through the

clear hull. Still the vessel hung in the water, not moving.

"Why isn't it responding?" muttered Max. "Don't they know us?"

"They should recognise us," said Lia. "After all, we saved their island from Finaria the Sea Snake."

"So why do I have a bad feeling about this?"

Just then, there was a flash from the hull of the battle sub, and a thick rubbery strand shot through the water. *Glue gun!* Max had no time for evasive action. The long sticky rope latched onto the aquasphere. It splattered like chewing gum across the plexiglass and set fast. Desperately, Max tried to fire his blasters, but they were covered in the glue. The escape hatch was clogged too. *There's no way out!*

The aquasphere began to move, tugged towards the battle sub by the sticky strand. Max leant on the thrusters until the engines screamed, but it was useless.

A flash of silver streaked down in front of the aquasphere. *Spike!* Lia was angled forward on Spike's back while the silver swordfish began to saw at the tether of glue. He worked quickly, but Max knew it wasn't enough. *The glue rope's too thick.*

"Get back, Lia!" Max called. "Once they take me to Gustados, General Phero will sort things out. I'll be free in no time."

"Phero might not still be in power," Lia reminded him.

"I'll have to take that chance," replied Max. "Just don't get captured – so you can rescue me if I need you!"

Lia gave a crooked smile. "I'll be here." She called Spike away from the rope, and they sank down into the gloom.

Moments later, Max realised he wasn't heading for Gustados. The battle sub was dragging the aquasphere away from the island, not towards it.

Max could see a dappling of sunshine through the water above him. *We're being pulled to the surface!*

The aquasphere broke through the top of

the water into daylight. Through the streaming plexiglass, Max could see the half-submerged battle sub in front of him. And in front of that was a wall of ice!

"Iceberg ahead, Max," warned Rivet.

Max bit his lip. "It doesn't make sense," he muttered. "Why are the Gustadians heading straight for it?" Max waited for the sub to change direction to avoid the berg, but the wall of ice grew closer and closer...

"Hang on, Riv. We're going to hit!" Max said.

Suddenly, the ice directly in front of the Gustadian sub slid smoothly aside to reveal a symmetrical opening.

Max held his breath as the battle sub slid through the doorway into the iceberg, followed by Max and Rivet, helpless in the aquasphere. "It's fake, Riv. That's why we couldn't see it when we were submerged – it doesn't drop far below the surface!"

Max checked out the inside of the iceberg, blinking against the glare of artificial lighting. The interior was hollow. For as far as he could see, there was a huge harbour criss-crossed with a grid of floating jetties. Military vessels of all shapes and sizes were moored. Some of them were painted in the Gustadians' trademark rainbow colours, but others were camouflaged. The walkways bustled with armed Gustadians.

Then Max caught sight of a line of arrow-shaped sails, and a chill sped down his spine. *Blade vessels!* The black, razor-winged craft were the same vessels that Kade's minions had used to attack Max and Lia outside Deepholm Temple.

The battle sub was pulling the aquasphere towards the docks. Max could see rows of rainbow banners hanging from the walls. The symbol they carried was big and bold –

a clenched fist over the letter K.

Max's stomach dropped. He had no doubt what K stood for. *Kade!*

"General Phero won't be able to help us here, Rivet. This place is full of Gustadians loyal to Kade!"

"Don't like it, Max," whined Rivet.

The aquasphere bumped against a jetty. A group of Gustadian soldiers roped it in and

fired narrow laser beams at the glue sealing
the hatch closed. Max felt the heat through
the double plexiglass walls. Moments later,
the soldiers wrenched open the hatch, and
Max found himself staring into the barrel
of a blaster. The Gustadian holding the gun
gestured with it towards the jetty.

*No point trying to fight now. Better to bide
my time…*

"Come on, Rivet. We're under orders," said Max, climbing out.

The dock swayed under Max's feet, bobbing on the pontoons that kept it afloat. Three soldiers were pointing their blasters straight at his head. And one soldier had taken hold of Rivet's collar, pressing his weapon against the dogbot's eye.

Rivet won't stand a chance if he takes a blast into his robobrain at point-blank range!

Just then a stern-looking Gustadian came forward, and the soldiers saluted. The newcomer was shorter than the others, but more heavily built, and there were brightly coloured ribbons attached to the shoulders of his silver uniform. *A high-ranking officer.*

"You, I believe, are Max, the meddling Aquoran boy," the officer said. "Welcome. Kade will be so pleased when he hears that I have captured you."

Max glared at him. "So who are you?"

"I am Lieutenant Harg," the Gustadian replied with a smirk and a slight bow. "And we are the future."

"The future?"

"Gustadians loyal to Kade, our true leader."

"What about General Phero?" asked Max.

Harg frowned. "Phero is weak. Only Kade is strong enough to defeat our enemies. He will lead us to total victory in the Delta Quadrant."

"But the civilisations of the Delta Quadrant aren't hostile. They're allies of Gustados."

"Really? Even now, Arctiria uses dark magic to spread its icy kingdom south."

Max almost laughed. "That's crazy. The Arctirians aren't magic. And besides, they want peace."

I can't imagine them going to war. They're far too vain to get their hands dirty in battle!

Harg snorted. He spoke quickly to his guards in a low voice and strode off. Two soldiers took hold of Max's arms, ready to drag him away.

I guess we're heading for the cells...

Just then there was a deep, bone-shaking rumble. *Wham!* The whole base convulsed. Immense waves surged across the harbour, and the walkway under Max's feet bucked and tilted. The men holding Max were fighting to keep their balance. Max used the moment to drive his elbows into their sides. The winded soldiers lost their footing and plunged into the sea.

Max dived towards Rivet, knocking against the legs of two more soldiers who had tried to lift the dogbot. The men overbalanced, arms windmilling, and then toppled into the sea after their comrades.

"Magnetise paws, Rivet!" Max said. Rivet's

paws hummed and stuck to the metal jetty. Max clung on to his dogbot with both hands.

The jetty lurched again. A huge wave smashed over Max's prone body, and his legs slid across the rolling deck. He fought to keep hold of Rivet as waves surged around them.

What on Nemos is happening?

CHAPTER THREE

THE MIGHTY FORTRESS

Wave after wave burst over the pitching jetty. Bits of the fake iceberg's walls rained down in clouds of spray and dust, splashing into the churning sea and bobbing on the surface.

Max lifted his head, cautiously. Something titanic was smashing into Kade's base. Through one of the gaping holes in the iceberg walls, Max glimpsed smooth black shapes hunched on the ocean surface.

What are they?

On the far side of the base, a huge head crashed through the wall of the iceberg, rising high above the surface of the water. It was grey, grooved and edged with warty nodules. It towered above the harbour, turning in the

air. Then a long narrow fin behind it lifted up, and the creature slammed back down onto the water.

Max felt a thrill of awed wonder. *A humpback whale!*

Another great wave swept across the harbour. Before it surged over Max, he saw something else. On the colossal creature's dark back, a tiny figure raised her spear triumphantly. *Lia!* Max saw a huge fluked tail lift and fall. It smashed a row of blade vessels down into the depths.

Rivet was still hanging on to the jetty with his magnetised paws. "Whales, Max," he said.

Max swallowed water, smiling. "Yes, Riv. Lia must have called them with her Aqua Powers."

Between the swelling waves, Max could see three humpback whales swimming inside the harbour. Smaller, black and white orcas dodged between them, snapping at the

Gustadians who had been thrown into the water. And somewhere in the middle, a flash of silver zipped through the water near Lia's humpback. *Spike!*

The Gustadians were panicking. They tried to run as the whales demolished their iceberg hideaway, but they couldn't stand upright on the walkways in the churning sea. The terrified soldiers lost their footing and fell, screaming, into the water.

Max looked for the aquasphere. Incredibly it was bobbing at the end of the jetty. *It's still attached to the battle sub by the glue rope.*

The whale with Lia on its back surfaced again. She was holding her fingers to her temples. *She's communicating with the whales.*

An orca surfaced near Max. It fastened a bright black eye on him and gave a high-pitched chuckle. Then it turned towards the aquasphere, opened its mouth to show two rows of sharp white teeth, and bit through the glue line.

"Thank you!" cried Max, and the orca spun away with a wave of its flipper.

Lia was waving urgently to Max. *She's saying we need to leave.* Max waved back. "Let's go, Riv!" They made a dash for the aquasphere. The whales had stopped making waves, so the walkway was steadier underfoot. Gustadians were trying to pull themselves out of the water onto the jetty, and Max felt fingers crunch under his foot as he ran. The Gustadian yelped, but Max didn't look back.

He leapt into the aquasphere, followed by Rivet, and started the engines.

The whales were heading out of the base's harbour. Max sped after them, avoiding the flailing bodies of Gustadians in the water. He piloted the little craft through one of the gaping holes in the walls, and back out into the ocean. Max glanced back and saw vessels pouring out of the damaged berg and scattering in different directions.

Max smiled to himself. *They'll have to build a new hideaway. That should keep Kade busy for a while!*

They raced north until Gustados was far out of sight, Max skimming the aquasphere over the surface of the ocean. Ahead, the whales slowed, then they began to dive, one by one. Max brought the aquasphere to a halt and watched. Soon the sea looked empty and calm. Suddenly, one of the humpbacks spouted, then another, and another. Max felt his heart soar at the sight of the three plumes of warm, wet breath shooting up from the ocean and cresting high in the air.

Rivet barked excitedly. Max let out a long breath. "Wow." He tipped the aquasphere down under the surface, and his heart leapt again. The undersea ocean was an orchestra of the long, haunting songs of the humpbacks and the clicks and trills of the orcas.

Lia was riding a humpback below Max. Spike swam beside her and Lia swung herself onto his back.

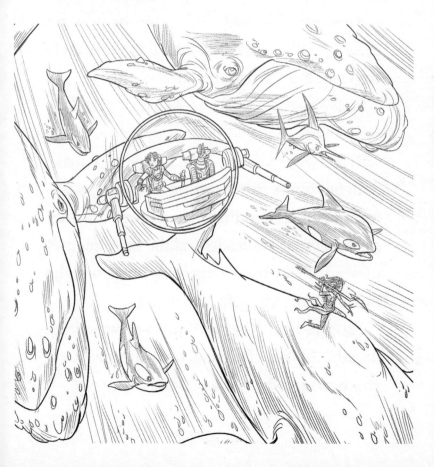

The humpbacks accelerated away, and the pod of orcas peeled off to the left. Max and Lia waved as they vanished into the gloom.

"Thanks, Lia," said Max. "You've totally destroyed Kade's rebel base."

"And all without the help of your Breather technology," replied Lia. Her face was glowing with excitement, and she couldn't stop smiling. "Whale-riding is the best!"

Spike rolled over in the water, tipping Lia off his back.

"Yikes! Sorry, Spike!" said Lia with a laugh, hanging on to his dorsal fin from below. "I mean apart from riding you, of course!" Spike righted himself and let Lia climb back on.

"We're lucky the whales were close enough to help," said Max, still chuckling.

Lia nodded. "They're only this far south because of the changing temperature. Did you find out what's happening?"

Max shook his head. "One of Kade's followers, Lieutenant Harg, thinks the Arctirians are using magic to freeze the ocean."

"That's crazy. The Arctirians are even less magical than you tech-obsessed Aquorans."

Max let the wisecrack pass. "Right. It must be something else. And I bet Kade's behind it."

They continued their journey northwards, eyes peeled for any more Gustadians on their tail, but, thankfully, there was no sign of any.

After a while, Lia pointed to something blue-white in the distance. Max strained his eyes. *It's too small to be an iceberg.*

As they got closer Max saw that it was a narrow shelf of ice on the surface of the sea. "It can't be Arctiria," he said to Lia. "And it isn't wide or deep enough to be an iceberg. Let's go up and look."

They surfaced and stared at the gleaming shape. It was a long peninsula of ice, thin at the edge, but thicker as it reached into the distance. Much further, in that direction, Max could see a tiny-looking icy peak. "That's Arctiria, off in the distance!" he said.

"We could walk all the way there on this ice floe," said Lia. "It's one long icy arm. But what's caused it?"

"I don't know," admitted Max. "Let's have another look from underneath."

Max piloted the aquasphere down, Spike and Lia following. But Rivet barked a warning.

"Big thing below, Max!"

Max and Lia looked down at the ocean floor, and Lia gave a cry. At first Max thought a mountain was scuttling along the bottom of the sea. Then he saw that the cone-shaped hulk wasn't quite that big.

It's about the size of an Aquoran battlecruiser!

Max gulped. Beneath the mountainous shell on its back, Max glimpsed swivelling eyes and antennae. The massive creature had jointed legs, churning up clouds of sand. It also had a seriously big pair of claws, coated in gleaming metal. The natural shell of the huge claws, legs and head was vivid red.

It's beautiful, thought Max. *Apart from its metal shell...*

The gigantic, conical shell on the creature's back was an ugly gun-metal grey, and it was covered with swivel-jointed weapons, including a huge cannon.

"It's one of the temple guardians," shouted Lia. "Shelka, the giant hermit crab!"

Max felt his stomach lurch. "Shelka the Robobeast. Kade must have made the guardian swap its own shell for this one. He's made a mighty, blaster-studded fortress!"

As the Robobeast scurried along the ocean floor, Max saw a small green stone flash on the red shell between its eyes. He pointed it out to Lia, who nodded. "The gemstone."

"If we can prise it out, we'll break Kade's control over the crab," said Max.

A volley of fire burst from Shelka's blasters. The shots tore through the water towards them. "Get back, Lia!" yelled Max, tugging back the controls and rolling the craft out of the way. He fired the aquasphere's guns.

His shot sliced through the top of one of Shelka's antennae. The Robobeast snapped its head and legs back, pulling them all the way into the metal shell. Suddenly, the more vulnerable parts of Shelka's body, and the gemstone, were all hidden inside its fortress. Max's fire sparked off it harmlessly.

"Keep it busy!" said Lia. "I'll go around the

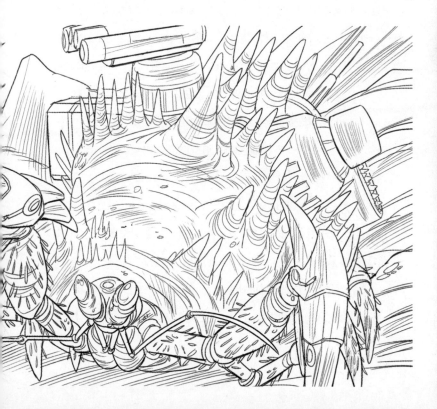

back and get the gemstone!"

"You can't reach the stone," argued Max. "It's inside the shell!"

"Stop firing when I'm in position," replied Lia. "I'll grab the stone when Shelka puts its head out."

Spike had already darted down towards the seabed. Max fired again, aiming for the dark, cave-like opening at the shell's base. He could just see Shelka's stalked eyes gleaming, but they were protected by the lip of the shell.

Spike swam in a wide circle and came to a stop just behind and above Shelka's hiding-place. Lia gave a thumbs-up to show she was in position. Max eased off the trigger.

Slowly, Shelka's claws emerged from the shell, followed by its jointed legs and flat head. *And the gemstone!*

Shelka's eyes fixed on Max. Spike moved forwards, carrying Lia closer. Lia drew her spear from her belt. Max's heart thumped as he watched Lia slide off Spike's back to stand lightly on Shelka's thick natural shell, behind its eyes. *He can't feel her,* Max realised, nerves clawing his stomach. Lia knelt, ready to prise out the stone with her knife...

With one sudden, smooth movement, Shelka withdrew its body into its metal fortress. *Crash!* Lia was flung backwards. The edge of the shell caught Lia on the back of her head. She catapulted off Shelka's back, and her body landed limply on the sea-floor.

Spike shot down to protect Lia, and Max loosed a volley of fire. But Shelka pounced, blocking the blaster fire with a metal claw then swiping Spike away. It reached down and picked up Lia.

Max didn't dare fire again. Helplessly, he watched Lia regain consciousness and stare straight into her captor's stony face.

CHAPTER FOUR

RUNAWAY SPHERE

The Robobeast held Lia close to its black eyes. Its long feelers twitched in front of grinding jaws as it studied her.

Lia struggled, pressing her hands against the edges of the pincers, trying to prise them apart. The crab kept on squeezing, tighter and tighter, and Max heard her groan. *It's playing with her!*

Max set the aquasphere on a direct course. "Rivet – hold her steady. I'm going out there."

"Careful, Max." Rivet took the steering lever in his iron jaws, holding it in position.

Max revved the engines and flung open the aquasphere hatch. He scrambled out, gasping as the cold seawater gushed over his gills. Crouching low, he kept his balance on top of the vessel as it sped towards Shelka.

Shelka swivelled its eyes at Max as he leapt off the aquasphere and landed in a crouch on the Robobeast's claw, just behind the pincer joint.

Lia looked up, her face pale. "Help me, Max," she whispered weakly.

He drew his hyperblade. The narrow vernium blade was so thin it was almost invisible from the side, but it was unbelievably strong.

Strong enough to open a crab claw, I hope!

Max aimed the tip of the blade at the notch nearest the joint of the claw, but the crab

swept its claw through the water and Max
fell, the blade missing its mark, rebounding
off the hard shell. Max regained his balance
and crouched lower. He steadied his hand…
He forced the blade downwards. This time
the hyperblade slid between the pincers.
Max tried to swivel it, grunting with effort
as the crab slammed him back and forth in
the water.

Lia moaned. Her head whipped from side to side as the crushing claw rattled her helpless body.

"Hang on, Lia," said Max. "Almost there..."

The hyperblade twisted abruptly, prising the claw apart a little. It was enough.

"Aahh!" Lia gasped for breath. She wriggled free and slithered down, out from between the pincers.

Spike was ready. He darted forwards with perfect timing and caught Lia as she dropped. Then he doubled back.

Max bent his legs, readying to leap. Spike swam past and Max jumped onto the swordfish's back, behind Lia. "Go, Spike!" he cried, and the brave swordfish sped off.

Shelka opened fire with all its shell cannon. Max and Lia hunched low to avoid the massive, boulder-sized bolts flashing past them as Spike carried them away.

When Max glanced back, he was surprised that the mountainous Robobeast wasn't chasing them. And as soon as they were out of range of its weapons, it stopped firing.

"That's weird. It's given up!" said Max. "It's like it doesn't want to leave this place..."

Lia shrugged. "Perhaps it knows it couldn't catch us. It can't scuttle around very fast with that heavy shell on its back."

Max wasn't so sure. He'd glimpsed something on the back of Shelka's metal shell, and it had looked a lot like a set of thrusters. *I think it could swim if it wanted!*

Suddenly, Max remembered Rivet. He looked around quickly. *Where did the aquasphere go after Riv steered me to the crab?*

Then he saw it, and his heart leapt into his throat. The aquasphere was disappearing into the distance.

"Rivet can't stop!" he cried.

"Quick, Spike!" said Lia. "After the aquasphere!"

Spike sped up, streaking along the icy wall of the peninsula. Lia's swordfish swam as fast as he could, but the aquasphere was going at full speed. The vessel stayed in view, but they got no closer. Max shivered inside his deepsuit. The freezing water got colder and colder, stinging his face and gills. Patches of luminescence stirred as they passed, and strange, solitary jellyfish floated by, flickering with cold blue lights and dragging tangles of thin tentacles.

We mustn't lose Rivet!

Somehow Spike kept going. The narrow ice floe seemed endless. And then, at last, Max noticed a dark glow in a patch of sea ahead. As they got nearer, the patch grew bigger, and Max realised that he was looking at the eerie blue light of the submerged part of an iceberg.

Arctiria!

Max leaned forwards. "Lia – we need more speed. Rivet's going to crash unless I get close enough to use my headset."

Lia put her fingertips to her temples. Max

felt Spike's exhausted muscles pulse as he made a final, huge effort to catch up.

At last they drew level with the aquasphere. Desperately, Max yelled into his headset, "Pull up, Riv!" Rivet's red eyes rolled towards him. Max shouted again, "Pull back on the lever!" *Does he understand me?*

The aquasphere tilted upwards. *Go, Rivet!*

Max watched the little vessel zoom upwards and vanish from sight through the top of the ocean. Spike followed it up, and Max's head broke through the surface into an icy gust of wind, just in time to see the aquasphere soar through the air and bump down on the shore. It skidded, spinning, across the ice, and hurtled into a mound of snow with a muffled whumph!

Beyond the snowdrift, the ice sloped up into the foothills of the frozen city of Arctiria.

Spike stopped swimming, his head

drooping with exhaustion as Max and Lia slid off his back. Lia laid her face against the swordfish's heaving side, muttering to him, while Max clambered out onto the silent shore. Sheltering his eyes against the biting wind, he raced towards the half-buried aquasphere. Anxiously, Max shoved the snowdrift off the hatch and hauled it open. "Rivet?"

"Here, Max." Rivet's head popped up. His red eyes were whirling and his metal tongue was lolling out of his mouth. Max lifted him out of the aquasphere onto the ice, and he stumbled for a few jerky steps before coming to a stop. "Circuits dizzy, Max," he whimpered.

Lia came running over the ice. "Spike needs to rest. How's Rivet?"

Max checked the dogbot's connections. "He's not badly damaged." He checked over the aquasphere, and patted Rivet's iron head. "Well done, Riv. You helped save Lia and got us to Arctiria, with the aquasphere all in one piece!" Rivet wagged his metal tail.

"But we didn't get the gemstone," Lia pointed out.

Max nodded grimly. "And we've seen how dangerous Shelka is. Its shell is blaster-proof. But we'll get that stone somehow!"

Suddenly, they were startled by the crackle of a loudspeaker followed by a clipped voice echoing over the ice. Max recognised the arrogant tone of an Arctirian.

"Don't move, intruder, or you'll be blasted to pieces!"

Max shielded his eyes to see a vehicle swooping silently down the ice mountain. *An Arctirian sledge!* The streamlined shape seemed to hover just above the ice, but Max caught a flash of metallic runners hidden beneath its curved flank.

Four Arctirians were sitting straight-backed inside. Their glowing blue faces looked like ice, and just as cold. To Max's surprise, they were holding blasters.

"Get down!" Max whispered urgently, and

he and Lia dived behind the mound of snow surrounding the aquasphere.

Lia shook her head, puzzled. "The Arctirians didn't have weapons the last time we were here. They were peaceful. Rude, but peaceful!"

"That's right," replied Max. "Maybe these are really Gustadians in disguise. Or they could be actual Arctirians, if Kade's turned them hostile."

The sledge loudspeaker sounded closer. "Show yourselves! Invaders must be destroyed, in the name of our illustrious empress!"

Lia hissed. "The empress has turned bloodthirsty? Last I heard, she was peace-loving."

"I bet it's not the real empress," Max whispered back. "In fact, I bet my whole Psychotic Sharks record collection that it's Kade in disguise!"

The thought of Kade in holographic disguise gave Max an idea. He reached through the hatch of the aquasphere and groped around. He lifted out two of the stealth suits that he'd taken from the Gustadians on Verdula.

Lia's eyes widened. "Good idea!"

They slipped into the suits. The legs were much too long, so they pushed the elasticated ankle holes up to their knees, under a curtain of extra material. The long sleeves ballooned around their arms, too. Lia batted folds of material out of the way to look at the control panel on her wrist. It had a small screen and a set of buttons. "How does it work?" she asked, jabbing at the buttons.

Max took a step back as Lia flickered and changed before his eyes. Suddenly, she was a monkey-like Verdulan, and then she was an Aquoran – *Councillor Glenon!* – and then –

Whoa! – she was a walrus!

"At least you don't look out of place on the ice," said Max. She turned her whiskery, tusked face towards him. "Sorry," he added hurriedly. "Hang on. There's a list of species in the controls."

"We know where you are," thundered the Arctirian with the loudspeaker. "You have five seconds to show yourselves, before we fire. A mound of snow won't stop our blasters... 5…4…3…"

Max's fingers flew over the controls, scrolling down the list of species on the little screen. He couldn't see the word 'Arctirian'.

Where is it…?

"2…1…"

CHAPTER FIVE

IMPOSTERS IN ARCTIRIA

"Time's up!" said the voice. "Blast them!"

Lia must have found the switch, because where she had been standing, Max saw a towering, blue-skinned Arctirian, wearing elaborate councillor's robes. She nodded to Max and stepped into the open.

"Oh!" said one of the Arctirians.

Max found the setting, activating his disguise. He followed Lia and saw the Arctirians on the sledge lowering their blasters.

"You are a long way from the city. Do you need assistance?"

Max nodded, afraid to speak. The Arctirian disguise projected around him was twice his height. He would be talking from its stomach.

The Arctirians invited them onto the sledge, moving aside respectfully while Max and Lia slid on board.

Max sat down. He watched the Arctirian driver press a switch and spin a steering lever on the sledge console.

Easy controls. We might need to use this to get back here.

The vehicle turned around and sped up the steep slope of the iceberg. The angles of the ice flashed rainbow colours in the sunshine, and the air was dry and crisp. Max sat back and enjoyed the exhilaration of the ride.

At last the path levelled off. The sledge swerved around a crest and passed under an arch of beautifully sculpted ice. They entered the main Arctirian city.

Max recognised it from their last visit. They'd fought Nephro the Ice Lobster here. The battle had smashed up the place, but there was no sign of damage now.

The city was crafted out of ice, forty storeys high. There were soaring spiked towers linked by bridges, gleaming avenues, and multi-level plazas accessed by curved staircases. All were smooth and deep blue. Max glimpsed wide openings to grand chambers and smaller entrances to gloomier tunnels. There were pillars and domes, and fountains where ice was carved to look like flowing water. Everything sparkled.

The sledge stopped in a great square. The buildings around the sides were ornately carved, with panels of thin ice for windows. The square was full of Arctirians. All of the

tall humanoids were impossibly beautiful,
with willowy limbs, long narrow heads and
wide-spaced eyes set in glowing blue skin.

It was just like Max's last visit, except last
time the Arctirians had been strolling around
admiring themselves. Now they were standing

in ranks, armed with blasters. Max noticed again that the weapons were all shapes and sizes. *I wonder where they got them?*

One of the Arctirians in the sledge gestured across the square. "You are just in time for the empress's war meeting at the council chamber."

Max hesitated, and the Arctirian pointed to Max's holographic robes. "Am I mistaken? You are councillors, are you not?"

Max nodded, hoping he looked haughty.

He and Lia stood and climbed out of the sledge as gracefully as they could. Max glanced around. A group of Arctirians wearing robes like theirs was walking under an archway. Max and Lia followed them.

They passed through a curtain of slender icicles sculpted into strings of tinkling beads, and entered a large hall. It had rows of benches around the sides, facing a gleaming white throne. Sitting on it, poker-backed and regal, was the tall, slim figure of the Arctirian empress. Max felt a surge of excitement. Surely the empress was Kade in disguise…

We've found him!

Max and Lia sat down on an icy bench. Every muscle in Max's body wanted to leap up and unmask Kade. He fought to keep still.

The empress spoke. "Welcome, councillors! My news is good. We have finished giving out weapons from the cavern of seized arms."

So that's where they got the blasters! Max and Lia had defeated the Robobeast Nephro using a rocket launcher and crossbow they'd found in the contraband cavern. The cave had been packed with weapons that the Arctirians had taken from anyone they found travelling near their ice island.

The empress continued. "Now we are almost ready to invade Gustados!"

Max flinched with shock and felt Lia do the same. *Has Kade kicked off a war already?*

The audience muttered uneasily. A councillor sitting in front of Max shuddered and murmured to his neighbour, "Does that mean we will have to actually touch the Gustadians?"

His companion's lip curled. "I hope not," he whispered. "They are so revoltingly ugly, I'm sure touching one would make me quite ill!"

One councillor stood up and spoke directly to the empress. "Excellency, this decision to go to war seems very sudden. The Alliance—"

The empress fixed him with her haughty gaze and snapped, "The Delta Alliance is falling apart. Gustados is hostile. We must strike the first blow. Now is the right time. The peninsula we are building with the freeze-ray has almost reached Gustados. Soon our army will to march across it and into enemy territory. The Gustadians think they have a powerful navy. But we will crush it!" She paused to stare around the hall. Nobody else spoke.

A smile crossed the empress's face. She stood up, raising her arms. "Mobilise the army!" The cheering in the hall was half-hearted.

Lia whispered, "The freeze-ray must be at the end of the peninsula."

Max nodded. "That's why Shelka didn't chase us. I bet Kade has him guarding it!"

Lia glanced at the empress. "She must be Kade."

"Agreed. We need to show the Arctirians he's an imposter," Max replied.

Lia nodded back. "Our cover will be blown, but so will Kade's. Let's do it!"

They leapt off their seats and charged towards the empress. Shocked, she dodged to one side. Lia missed altogether, and Max's shoulder hit a glancing blow. He stumbled away, as shouts went up from other Arctirians. Max turned back and stared in confusion.

The empress's holographic disguise had flickered briefly, revealing the true appearance of the person behind. But the snarling face topped by long black hair didn't belong to Kade. It was someone Max knew all too well.

Cora Blackheart!

CHAPTER SIX

EMPRESS CORA

Max faltered. In an eyeblink, the Arctirian empress was back, looking solid and as large as life.

"It's Cora," said Lia, drawing her spear. Max had fought the deadly pirate many times. The last time he'd defeated her was during the battle with Jandor the Arctic Lizard. After that, he'd handed Cora over to the Arctirians. She'd been carted her off to be displayed in a tank as an art exhibit in the servants' quarters.

The tall blue figure pulled back the sleeve of her robe to look at a watch-like device on her wrist. Max recognised it – it was exactly the same as the one Kade had worn.

Kade must have freed Cora. Now she's working for him!

Cora pressed a button on the watch. There was a loud gasp from the Arctirians. With a shock, Max watched the hologram surrounding Lia dissolve. He looked down at himself and saw that his own disguise had gone, too.

Cora's watch must be able to control other stealth suits!

The Arctirians were shouting, outraged at the sudden appearance of two strangers at their council. "Wait!" Max said. "We are here on a mission. This person is not your empress. She is an imposter..."

The voices swelled again. "Absurd!"

"Ridiculous!"

Lia shouted. "It's true! Listen to him!"

But it was no good. Cora was chuckling. "A foolish claim! Everyone can see that I am the true empress." She clapped her hands and shouted, "Seize them!"

Max and Lia ran for it. They darted across

the council chamber before anyone could block their way. They hurtled through the ice curtain and out into the square. "Head for the sledge," yelled Max.

They could hear footsteps pounding after them, and shouts of "Stop them!"

Shocked Arctirians in the square reached out, reluctantly, to grab Max and Lia. But the elegant humanoids flinched aside at the last moment, with horrified murmurs. "Urgh," said one. "I can't touch that!" The path cleared as the Arctirians scurried out of their way.

Max and Lia ran to the sledge. Max dived into the driver's seat, while Lia jumped beside him. He slammed the starter button and swung the sledge around, out through the city archway. Howls of rage faded behind them.

"Thank Thallos they're too fussy to touch us!" Lia said, panting.

Max steered the sledge down the steep icy slope. From this height, he could see the long white ribbon of the peninsula snaking across the sea into the distance. "I hope Rivet's okay and still guarding the aquasphere," he muttered to Lia. "We need to get to the end of the peninsula quickly to destroy the freeze-ray."

"Before it completes the walkway," finished Lia.

Max nodded. "We've got to stop the Arctirian army marching across to attack Gustados!"

Max sledged to the foot of the icy mountain and skidded to a stop at the peninsula. He leapt out and dashed around the mound of snow. The aquasphere was right where they'd left it by the snowdrift, with Rivet standing guard.

"Max!" Rivet barked. "Rivet watched sphere!"

"Well done, Riv! Good job!" said Max, giving his dogbot's iron head a pat.

Lia ran to the edge of the ice and called to Spike. The swordfish answered with a trill, his dorsal fin breaking the surface of the water.

Max leaped through the aquasphere's entry hatch, Rivet bounding in after him.

Lia was already on Spike's back. "Ready when you are," she called.

Max switched the controls into land propulsion, and the aquasphere began to roll smoothly over the ice like a ball. Max's seat stayed upright as the pod spun around its axis.

Max waved to Lia. "We're off!" He sped down the narrow peninsula, with Spike and Lia swimming alongside. It was flat and featureless, and as Max rolled the aquasphere along it, he began to think about what was at

the end of it… The freeze-ray. And Shelka,
lurking below. An idea sparked in his mind.
Perhaps we can use one against the other.

Max turned to speak to Lia, coasting
through the waves. "I think we should try to
turn the freeze-ray on Shelka. A blast of ice

might slow it down long enough for us to get the stone and break Kade's control over it."

Lia grinned. "Nice thinking!"

At last Max saw the freeze-ray ahead, a few metres from the end of the ice, and surrounded by a few Arctirians. Max put on the brakes. "Slow down, Lia. We're nearly there," he warned.

Max edged closer. The freeze-ray looked like a squat, silver tower on wheels. He could see an arm-like nozzle at the top, with an Arctirian sitting behind it. *The controller.*

As Max watched, the device began to move. It rumbled over the ice and stopped nearer the edge. The controller tilted the nozzle, and a white ray burst out of it and flowed in a wide beam onto the waves. At the touch of the energy beam, the water expanded into ice with a splintering sound. It became a smooth white surface, extending the end of the peninsula.

Neat, thought Max. *And effective.* The black rocky island of Gustados was visible in the distance. *At this rate, the peninsula will reach it very soon.*

Max turned to speak to Lia but caught sight of something in the distance which made his heart hammer. An aquabike was speeding towards them, ridden by what looked like the Arctirian empress. *Cora!*

Max's eyes widened, stomach sinking with dread. Behind Cora, Max could see a line of marching Arctirians. "Arctirian soldiers," he yelled to Lia. "Heading this way!"

CHAPTER SEVEN

SKI-SLOPE SHELKA

"Let's go!" yelled Max. But just as he was about to gun the thrusters towards the ray, the ice rumbled beneath the aquasphere.

Crash!

The ice floe in front of Max shattered in an explosion of flying shards. The aquasphere lifted and rolled backwards. "Hold on, Riv!" muttered Max, as he steadied the vessel. Then he saw what had burst through the ice before them...

Shelka!

The metal shell loomed up higher and higher, trailing seaweed, until the whole grey mountain gleamed dully in the sunshine. At the shell's base, Shelka's legs scrabbled at the ice. Its crazed, stalked eyes swivelled towards Max, and its metal claws opened

wide enough to crunch a battlecruiser. Max could hear the shocked cries of the Arctirians from the freeze-ray on the other side of the monster, but Shelka blocked his path.

If I can keep it focused on me, Lia might have time to reach the ray.

The Robobeast snapped one giant claw at the aquasphere. Max veered sideways, but the second claw slammed down in front of him, blocking his path. Max slammed on the brakes, thrown forward in his seat as they skidded to a stop.

The shadow of Shelka's second claw spread over the aquasphere. Rivet whined. *Shelka's going to crush us.*

The claw reached down and grasped the aquasphere. But instead of crushing the hull, the aquasphere popped free like a pea from a pod. Max clung on as the orb vessel soared into the air, arcing over the Robobeast's shell.

The aquasphere was never meant to fly!

Max caught a glimpse of Lia. She was riding Spike near the shore trying to reason with the Arctirians by the freeze-ray. But a tall blue creature was pointing the nozzle straight at Lia.

Bang! The aquasphere landed on Shelka's conical shell. The blow flung Max forwards against his seat straps and his head snapped back painfully. Rivet gave a startled bark as he tumbled off the seat. "Upside-down, Max!"

The cockpit seat righted itself and Max steered the aquasphere down the other side of the hermit crab's slippery metal shell, rolling faster and faster. He saw Lia gawp at the sight of him then spur Spike on towards the ray. The Arctirians in control of the freeze-ray had abandoned the device. Shelka's attack had almost broken off the tip of the peninsula, and they were too busy panicking about being stranded to care about anything else.

"Danger, Max," said Rivet. Max swerved desperately to avoid Shelka's blasters flaring in their path like exploding slalom poles. The aquasphere rolled off the base of the metal shell and landed with a skidding thump on the peninsula.

Without pausing, Max accelerated across the fractured ice towards the ray. Suddenly, he heard another great crash, and a long *CRAAAAAACK!*

He glanced back. The monstrous hermit crab was hammering the ice floe with a claw. A long crack opened up, then spread quickly towards Max.

Rivet barked, "Trench, Max!" The crack reached the aquasphere and disappeared under it.

Uh, oh!

Max's stomach lurched as the aquasphere

dropped like a stone in an avalanche of ice, and crashed into the churning ocean.

The aquasphere thrusters were firing on all cylinders, and the vessel's land-mode was still rotating it. Instead of whizzing smoothly through the water, the aquasphere spun in a dizzying spiral.

Max shook his head, trying to focus. He switched the aquasphere to water mode and squinted through the clearing bubbles.

Where's Shelka?

A shadow appeared out of the gloom. Max jumped, and then breathed a sigh of relief. Lia and Spike! But Lia was waving, wildly.

"Look out, Max!" she cried, pointing urgently over his shoulder.

Max whirled around. The dark blue shadow of what was left of the peninsula loomed above them on the ocean surface.

But under the peninsula, the mountainous bulk of Shelka hung in the sea. The Robobeast was watching them. Its blasters had stopped, and it wasn't moving, but Max could see churning water behind and below it.

Its thrusters are keeping it afloat. It's treading water!

There was a muffled splash and rush of

bubbles as something dived into the water nearby.

"Bike, Max," warned Rivet.

"I see it, Riv," replied Max. "And I see who's on it!"

A woman was sitting on the aquabike. She had an Amphibio mask clamped to her face and a mad black halo of floating hair. One leg was encased in a long black boot, and the other was a silver robotic peg-leg. *Cora Blackheart! She's dropped her disguise now the Arctirians can't see her.*

Cora swished the cat-o'-nine-tails she always carried. The electric lashes cracked, sending sparks arcing across the water.

"Ahoy there, sea scum. I'm back!"

Cora brought the aquabike to a sudden halt next to Shelka. She climbed onto Shelka's claw, leaving the bike to drift slowly down to the bottom of the sea. Cora swaggered along the crab's claw, then sat down on the Robobeast's back. She ran a black-nailed finger over the green stone.

"I expect you're wondering what I'm doing here," she said. "Well, as you know,

those stupid Arctirians made me into an art piece. They came and pointed at me, throwing insults and raw fish." Cora's eyes flashed and she breathed deeply through the Amphibio mask. "They should have known better than to mess with me, the fools. Once Kade freed me from that stupid tank, and recruited me to his cause, I could walk among them and make them pay!"

Max waited silently, hoping the pirate might give away Kade's whereabouts. *Tell us something useful, Cora!*

Cora kept gloating. "I've been impersonating the empress for a month, wearing one of Kade's stealth suits. Under my orders the Arctirians built the freeze-ray, using Kade's brilliant design, and leaving Shelka under my control, too. The Lord of Illusion is a technological genius! You have no hope of stopping him."

"Don't be too sure," said Lia angrily, but Cora just laughed.

"Oh, you can't imagine his cunning, pulling the strings from his Maze of Illusion. War is coming! And we will conquer the entire Delta Quadrant! I will rule at his side. We will have ultimate power, and riches beyond count."

Cora stared at Max with her cold dark eyes, and smiled like a shark behind the Amphibio mask. "But first, you two meddling urchins must die..."

CHAPTER EIGHT

ICED CRAB

Max tore his eyes away from the crazed pirate. "Make for the freeze-ray," he said to Lia through his headset. "Fire it when I lead Shelka into position!"

Lia nodded. "Be careful!" She whirled away on Spike.

The crab lunged after Max, claws snapping. He gunned the aquasphere in the opposite direction.

"Crab after us, Max!" said Rivet.

"That's the plan, Riv." Max glanced back.

Shelka moved fast, despite its colossal shell. Cora urged it on with her whip, lashing the crab's head with a burst of sparks.

Max swerved the aquasphere, doubling back towards the peninsula. He could feel the water surging from between Shelka's snapping claws. The ice wall loomed ahead.

Almost there...

Smash! Shelka swung a claw against the aquasphere, batting it against the ice with a crunch. Max's temple bounced painfully off the plexiglass.

"Fire the energy cannon!" shouted Cora. A huge cannonball of energy hurtled in Max's rear viewer and Max dipped the sub, narrowly avoiding the blast. Volley after volley of energy bolts flashed past him and smashed into the ice, carving dozens of craters and tearing off great chunks with a sound of thunder.

"Scared, Max," Rivet whimpered.

"I know, Riv. Hang on," replied Max, fighting with the controls. They'd almost reached the end of the peninsula.

I hope Lia's there...

Crash! A blaster bolt slammed into the aquasphere's primary engine. The lights flickered off and the vessel lurched to a shuddering stop.

Max thumped the console. "We've lost power!" Panic seized him. *We're sitting ducks!* Max thought fast. He turned to his dogbot. "I need you to take me up to the surface, then head for the ray, as fast as you can."

"Yes, Max."

Max opened the hatch, and Rivet surged out and up. Shelka's blasters had made the sea a jumble of icy fragments. Max heard Cora's frustrated cries from somewhere below. "Come back here, you filthy maggot, or you'll regret it!"

She's lost us in the debris!

Max's head broke the surface. The freeze-ray was directly ahead. Propellers whirring, Rivet dragged Max to the peninsula, boosting them up onto the ice with a burst of thruster-power. "Thanks, Riv!"

Behind him, Max saw the legion of Arctirian soldiers marching onto the narrow bridge of ice left by Shelka's attack. *They're heading for Gustados.* Max clambered to his feet and set off running towards the ray. The Arctirians in charge of the ice weapon were shaking their hands and robes in disgust and shouting, "The nasty little sea-creature touched me!"

Max almost smiled. The 'nasty little sea-creature' was sitting at the top of the tower, moving a joystick at the controls, while Spike bobbed in the water nearby.

"Lia!" Max shouted. "Get ready to fire!"

As he spoke, a wave of seawater surged over the ice. Shelka scuttled out of the ocean to the side of Max. From her perch on its back, Cora pointed at Max, shrieking, "Crush him!"

Shelka lifted its claws, streaming seawater. Rivet stopped and growled at the crab. The huge Robobeast paused, and its eyes swivelled down to focus on the dogbot.

"Not the piddling robot!" screamed Cora. "Crush the boy!"

"Now!" Max yelled to Lia, rolling sideways. A blast of unbelievable cold shot past Max's ear with a deafening hiss. He lifted his head to see Lia firing the freeze-ray like a hosepipe, steadily covering the Robobeast in a layer of ice. From the tip of its shell down to the ends of its claws, it froze like a statue on a plinth.

With a cry of horror, Cora flung herself off Shelka's back just before the ice reached her. She landed in a crumpled heap on the ice.

Lia pointed the freeze-ray at her. "Don't move a muscle!" Rivet moved to stand guard over Cora too, growling deep in his throat. The pirate scowled, but stayed very still.

Max ran to the Robobeast and grasped a claw. It was slick with ice. Gritting his teeth against the freezing chill that bit into his fingers, he climbed up onto Shelka, careful not to slip off the huge frozen creature. Max drew his hyperblade as he made it to the crab's head. He spotted the green gemstone sparkling beneath the frost between Shelka's eyes. He levered his blade under the gemstone, and it popped out into his hand.

"Watch out, Max!" called Lia, from the freeze-ray controls. "Shelka's thawing."

Max slid down the crab's slippery metal shell, as Shelka trembled beneath him. He jumped clear.

Snap! The ice covering the robotic shell fractured all over, like shattered glass.

Slowly, Shelka began to twitch. A layer of ice fell off the beast's stalked eyes, then from its quivering feelers. Shelka shook a mini-avalanche off its legs, and then its claws. It gave a great shudder, and the ice sealing it into the metal shell exploded in a cascade of flying shards.

Shelka stripped the metal casing from its claws. Then Max watched, awed, as the giant crab glided out of the metal shell Kade had constructed for it. Its own soft, curled abdomen had no armour. Without its fortress, Shelka was no longer a Robobeast. The temple guardian was finally free.

"Woooo! Go, Shelka!" called Lia.

Its stalked eyes turned on its former prison. Suddenly, it swung one of its giant pincers, smashing it into the empty metal shell. It skidded along the ice, then splashed into the sea, soaking the Arctirian soldiers. The ranks of blue creatures had been watching silently, faces etched with horror, but when the freezing water hit them, they started to howl with shock and disgust.

Lia waved as the freed crab slid into the water. "Bye!" she shouted. A moment later, the temple guardian was gone. "Shelka thanked us for our help," Lia said to Max. "It's going home to the temple, where it left its own shell. It will return to sleep."

Max nodded, feeling a swell of pride at having helped to free another noble creature.

The Arctirians were crowding closer. Max pointed at Cora. "This person has tricked you and your people." He lifted Cora's sleeve and pressed a button on her watch. The Arctirians gave a horrified gasp as Cora disappeared, replaced by the figure of their empress. Max switched off the stealth suit, and Cora reappeared, scowling at all the blasters suddenly pointing at her. "Stupid Arctirians. I'll get you for this, Max!"

The Arctirians held their weapons in trembling hands, shaking their heads.

"This ugly woman?"

"How could we think she was our divine empress?"

"Why didn't we notice the horrible stench?"

Max grinned. "Tell us where you've hidden the real empress, Cora. I'm sure I can persuade the Arctirians to put you in a bigger tank if you cooperate. Or a

smaller one if you don't..."

Cora's frown deepened, but Max could see she was beaten, for the moment. "She's in a cave," she muttered. "I'll show them where."

"Very wise," said Max. He turned away from the sulking pirate. "That was good shooting," he said to Lia, with a grin. "Now, can you help me retrieve the aquasphere? I need to get that engine fixed!"

CHAPTER NINE

ON WITH THE QUEST

Max picked up a delicate crystal goblet, taking care not to touch the waiter's blue hand when he lifted it off the ornate tray. The Arctirian looked relieved as he backed away to offer the tray to other guests.

Lia clinked glasses with Max and took a sip of the neon blue drink. Max drank some of his, blowing away the wisps of violet fog that wafted off the surface. It was so cold it stung, and it tasted salty.

"I hope Spike's okay," whispered Lia. The swordfish was in a special tank, being pampered by adoring Arctirians who thought he was the most beautiful creature they'd ever seen.

"His only danger is that he'll become as vain as his admirers!" replied Max, with a grin. "Rivet's with him. He'll make sure he's safe."

Max gazed around the icy splendour of the Palace Court council room. They were sitting around a dazzling white table surrounded by Arctirian nobles, who all kept sneaking uncomfortable glances at Max and Lia.

The real empress was at the head of the table. She called for silence and lifted her goblet of cold, smoking liquid in a toast to Max and Lia. "To our saviours!"

There was a subdued chorus of "Hear, hear."

Max and Lia bowed politely, and the
empress continued. "But for Max and Lia,
I would still be Kade's captive." She looked
around sternly. "The criminal illusionist
disguised himself as my servant. He tricked

me into telling him where the pirate was, and then he freed her and captured me. They threw me into a filthy cave for almost a month." She shivered, then forced a smile. "But now I am back here with you. And the hideous pirate is back in her secure tank. The housekeepers can go and gawp at her whenever they wish."

The empress smiled again and continued. "In addition, the freeze-ray has been destroyed. The peninsula is thawing and the sea temperature is slowly returning to normal."

The Arctirians clapped, enthusiastically. The empress waited for the applause to die away, then continued speaking. "However, not all is well. Regrettably, we cannot yet disband our new army."

There were surprised mutters among the gathering. The empress raised her voice. "Of course we all agree that conflict is against our nature. However, desperate times call for desperate measures. There are still hostilities in the Delta Quadrant. We must be prepared."

Max felt worry clawing at his stomach. So much had gone well. He and Lia had defeated Shelka, and stopped the imminent war between the Arctirians and Gustadians, and returned Cora to captivity. But Kade was still out there, working his tricks as the Lord of Illusion. Peace could only be restored when he was captured.

We need to prove he was the slippery villain who planted the bomb at the Alliance conference. That's the only way the Alliance members will go back to trusting each other.

Max was relieved when the empress's speech was over and the Arctirians began to talk among themselves, so that he and Lia could slip away from the table.

"I'll be glad to leave the frosty old Arctirians behind us," whispered Lia.

"Me, too," said Max. "Now that I've fixed the aquasphere, I want to get away as soon as possible. We've got a quest to finish."

"To find Kade," added Lia. "And retrieve my mother's ring."

"It's not going to be easy."

Lia chewed her lip. "But Cora did give us a clue. Remember what she said about Kade's 'Maze of Illusion'?"

"She said Kade was pulling the strings from the Maze of Illusion."

"Could that be where he's hiding?" Lia asked, and Max nodded.

"Yes, it must be his headquarters. After all, he calls himself the 'Lord of Illusion.'"

"So, when we find it, he'll be there!"

"That's right," replied Max. "And if anyone can track down Kade in his maze, it's you and

me." He whacked Lia's web-fingered hand in a high-five, and they grinned at each other.

"On with the quest!"

THE END

Don't miss Max's next Sea Quest adventure,
when he faces

HYDROR
THE OCEAN HUNTER

978 1 40834 097 4

WIN AN EXCLUSIVE GOODY BAG

In every Sea Quest book the Sea Quest logo is hidden in one of the pictures. Find the logo in this book, make a note of which page it appears on and go online to enter the competition at

www.seaquestbooks.co.uk

We will be picking five lucky winners to win some special Sea Quest goodies.

You can also send your entry on a postcard to:

Sea Quest Competition,
Orchard Books, Carmelite House
50 Victoria Embankment
London EC4Y 0DZ

Don't forget to include your name and address!

GOOD LUCK

Closing Date: 31st October 2016

IF YOU LIKE SEA QUEST, YOU'LL LOVE BEAST QUEST!

Series 1: COLLECT THEM ALL!

An evil wizard has enchanted the magical beasts of Avantia. Only a true hero can free the beasts and save the land. Is Tom the hero Avantia has been waiting for?

978 1 84616 483 5

978 1 84616 482 8

978 1 84616 484 2

978 1 84616 486 6

978 1 84616 485 9

978 1 84616 487 3